The Sillycone Family
(They like to line up!)

Anna, Mrs. Luigi, Mr. Luigi, Alex, and **Roberta**
(Mrs. Luigi makes pizza; Mr. Luigi makes ice cream.)

Noah
(The tropical fisherman)

Roshan and **Maria**
(The traffic policeman
and his police horse)

This is Migloo.

And this is the story of Migloo's weekend.

Benny and **Aki**
(Benny doesn't do much.)

Molly
(She makes orange juice.)

Hannah
(She's the vet.)

Juan and **Conchita**
(He goes down manholes;
she goes up telephone poles.)

Lotti and **Noggin** and **Kitty** and **Toto**
(Noggin thinks he's a Viking, and Kitty thinks she's a cat.)

Reg
(He sells fruit and veggies.)

Boris
(He puts up posters.)

Mrs. Pankhurst
(and Henrietta)

Mia
(She can fly!)

Charlie
(The newspaper man)

Dr. Whom
(She is Sunnytown's doctor.)

Mr. Brush
(The musical brush seller)

Farmer Tom and **Suki**
(From Sunnytown Farm)

Terry and **Bea** and **Lizzy**
(Terry and Bea run Sunnytown's taxi service.)

Miss Othmar
(She is a teacher.)

Flossy
(The cotton-candy and
popcorn seller)

William Bee

Flashy Gordon
(The great film star)

Eric and **Ernie**
(Brother builders)

Mr. Tati and **Hulot**
(He sells all sorts of balloons.)

Mr. Tompion
(The clock winder)

Zebedee
(The costume-shop man)

Mr. and **Mrs. Dickens**
(He sells books and she teaches with them.)

Harry and **Alphonso**
(The Sunnytown firefighters)

Freda and **Bobby** and **Olivia** and **Bert**
(From the Sunnytown garage)

François and **Agatha**
(They deliver the mail.)

Mr. McGregor and **Rose**
(They grow lots of plants.)

Mr. and **Mrs. Smudge** and **Scruff**
(The messiest family in town)

Daisy and **Felix** and **Amit**
(They make sandwiches and sell carpets.)

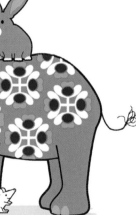

Otto
(and Robin)

Indira
and **Flopsy** and **Tiny Mouse**

Monsieur Pompidou and **Signor Uffizzi**
(The museum curators)

Lenny
(He sweeps up.)

Isabella and **Audrey**
(The traffic policewoman and police horse)

Noriko
(The local photographer)

Sydney and **Lily** and **Florence**
(Sydney is the window washer,
and Florence bakes bread.)

Migloo's Weekend

william bee

It's Saturday morning! Migloo is up nice and early, and he's ready for his breakfast!

"Mrs. Luigi's new café opens today, Migloo! Would you like a lift?" asks Noah. Migloo wags his tail, which means "I certainly do! I've been looking forward to it ever so much!"

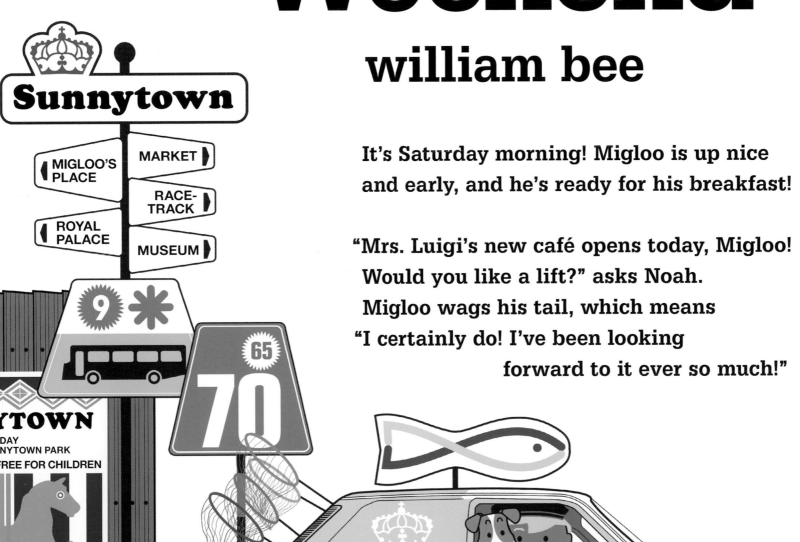

AT THE MARKET

Oh dear, just look at that line!
Migloo is far too hungry to wait! Luckily, his
friend Hannah comes to the rescue.
"Come on, Migloo, I know somewhere to get
a very good breakfast!"
Migloo wags his tail, which means "LET'S GO!"

AT SUNNYTOWN FARM

LOOK! It's Sunnytown Farm! There's Reg picking up some fresh, crunchy carrots, and Mr. Luigi is collecting tubs of lovely fresh cream. And—YUCK!—there's the stink of Audrey and Maria's freshly made manure! But where is Farmer Tom? And, more importantly, *where* is Migloo's breakfast?

Mrs. Dickens doesn't actually know how to drive a race car, but that's OK. She's got a book to teach her: *How to Drive a Race Car Without Hitting Anything.*

Migloo's been so busy being a mechanic . . .

that he's forgotten to have his lunch! So he makes a quick pit stop with Daisy, Felix, and Amit for a sandwich.

Uh-oh! Suki can't get her race car to start, not even with
Bert and Freda and Olivia helping.
But she has an idea!

"Quick, Tom! Quick, Migloo! Help me take all the go-faster
parts off my race car, and we'll put them on my Super
Sizzling Sausage car!" Migloo wags his tail, which means
"Good thinking, Suki!"

AT THE STARTING LINE

Suki's Sausage car really does look like a race car now! "Do you want to come for a ride, Migloo?" she asks.

Migloo slowly wags his tail, which means "OK. But are you *sure* this thing is safe?"

The lights are red. . . . The lights are green. . . . *GO! GO! GO!* Suki races away in a cloud of flames, smoke, and sizzling sausages!

? QUESTION ? TIME

Can you spot Batty?
Who has an orange juice?
Can you see Little White Owl?

William Bee's Busy Page

Sunnytown is such a busy place, *especially* on the weekend. There are lots and lots of people out and about shopping, eating, driving, playing, and seeing the sights—which means there are lots and lots of things for YOU to look for!

Look at all these logos. Whose are they?

1  **2** **3** **4**

5  **6**  **7**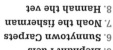

8

Who's going racing?

1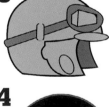

2

3

4

5

6

7

Who's hiding in Zebedee's costume shop car?

There are 25 toy Martians to find. Have you spotted them all? (Including this one!)

Noriko is always taking photos. Can you find where she took these?

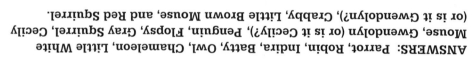

Whose mustache is Migloo wearing?

1  **2**  **3**  **4**  **5**  **6**

Mia is hovering and putting up light bulbs. But which one comes next?

She needs a white one next.

1 2 3 4 5 6 7 8 9 10 11 12 13 14 15 16

There seem to be ostriches everywhere! How many did you see?

William Bee counted 24 (including this one).

Who do these belong to?

1. Lotti 2. Alex 3. Noriko 4. Scruff 5. Olivia 6. Felix 7. Mr. Tompion 8. Miss Othmar 9. Hulot 10. Lily 11. Anna 12. Hannah 13. Lizzy 14. Harry and Alphonso 15. Mr. McGregor 16. Toto

There are TWO snails hidden in this whole book. And they look just like these.

Look at this crazy car! It's made up of NINE different vehicles. Can you tell what they are?

The blue racing wing is from Amit's race car. It's attached to the back of Bert and Freda's tow truck. Underneath is Sydney's motorbike sidecar. Those great big wheels are from Sunnytown Museum's steam engine. The cab is from the school bus, and the front door is from Noah's car. The fire engine. The front is from Hannah's car, and *right* at the front is the pointy nose of Sunnytown School's race car.

What is the scarecrow wearing?

Mr. Smudge's hat, Mr. Dickens's glasses, Monsieur Pompidou's shirt and tie, Boris's overalls, Noriko's buttons, and Noggin's golden boot!

On the pages where you see William Bee holding his yellow QUESTION TIME sign, it means there are LOTS of things to find!

And if you feel like getting even BUSIER, you can find the answers to ALL the questions he asks below on EACH of the 7 pages where his yellow QUESTION TIME sign appears!

So, that means you can find Flopsy 7 times and missing shoes in 7 different places! And lots of people eating carrots, wearing glasses, and swapping hats! Phew . . . that IS busy!

Busy Bee Questions

Here are all the things to find and how many times to find them in total!

How many times can you spot Roberta's little wheelie cat?

We counted 12 times (including this one).

Who's reading? (14) Who's on a ladder? (21) Who's holding a wrench? (24) Who has lost a shoe? (7) Who's holding candy or ice cream? (40) Who has a carrot? (29) Who's wearing glasses? (71) Apart from Mr. Tati and Hulot, who's holding a balloon? (8) Who has an orange juice? (27) **CAN YOU SEE:** Migloo? (7) Tiny White Mouse and Tiny Brown Mouse? (7 each) A rubber duck? (7) An ostrich egg? (12) Cecily and Gwendolyn? (7 each) Indira? (7) Batty? (7) Red Squirrel and Gray Squirrel? (7 each) Little White Owl? (7) Penguin? (7) Mr. Smudge—or just his sooty brush? (7) Flopsy? (7) Parrot? (7) Robin? (7) Chameleon? (7) The pesky leprechaun? (7) Who has swapped hats? What do Mr. Tati's balloons spell? What's the time? What have the two toucans taken?

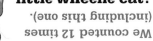